THE HUNGRY LADY AND THE BEAR

WRITTEN BY **RHYS GRIFFIN**

ILLUSTRATED BY **RACHEL JOANNA**

Published by Orange Hat Publishing 2021
ISBN 9781645382447

For information, please contact:
Orange Hat Publishing
www.orangehatpublishing.com
Waukesha, WI

Once upon a time, there was an old lady that
lived in the deepest, darkest part of the woods.
Every day, she would try to snatch up
innocent animals for supper.

This lady, however, was not very smart. She knew nothing about animals and thought catching them would be easy.

Whenever she needed a rabbit's foot, the rabbit would go straight into its hole and never come out.

When she craved turtle soup, the turtles would snap at her.

And whenever she wanted alligator tail, the alligators would chase her up a tree.

Every time, she would give up and settle for growing disgusting vegetables in her garden.
Yuck!

One day, the lady ran out of vegetable seeds. She began to grow very hungry, and craved something larger than usual. She looked through her cookbook and found a recipe for something called a Bear Claw. "Hmm," the lady thought. "Now that is something I've never had before! This will do nicely!"

So the lady grabbed her nets and traps and set out to catch the bear.

The lady searched high
and low for a bear to find.
She checked the brightest and
darkest parts of the woods, but she
could not find anything.

"I'm not giving up today," she said.
"I will find a bear, and it will be mine!"

As the old lady went further into the woods, she came across a set of footprints and a warning sign. The sign read, "DANGER! BEWARE OF THE BEAR!"

"Silly old sign," said the lady, "I'm not scared of any bears."

The lady followed the footprints to a deep, dark cave.
Inside the cave, there lay a gigantic sleeping grizzly
bear. The bear was big and brown, and snored loudly.

"Aha!" the lady whispered. "This is going to be easier than I thought!"

The lady grabbed her biggest net and swiped it over the bear.

The bear stood up and yawned.

ROAR!

"ROAR!" the bear growled as he awoke.

"Eek!" cried the lady.

The bear looked down at the lady. He was very grumpy.

"Who are you?" he growled. "And why have you woken me up?"

The lady trembled. "E-e-excuse me, Mister Bear," she said nervously, "I was just looking for a bear claw, and I was wondering if . . . I could have one of yours?"

The bear leaned in close to the lady.

"So," he trembled, "you're the one that's been trying to snatch up all my animal friends. You, lady, are very cruel indeed. Do you really think we're going to let you eat us?"

The lady began to cry.

"I'm sorry, Mister Bear!" she sobbed. "I've run out of food. I'm tired of eating vegetables all the time, and I want to eat something different. I never realized that eating other animals was a mean thing to do! I just want to eat something good!"

The bear thought for a moment. "I see," he said. "Well, there is a way to eat meat without hurting other animals."

The bear went to his kitchen in the back of his cave and looked. He returned with a small box. "What are those?" asked the lady.

"These are meat seeds," said the bear. "I like a big, juicy fish myself, or some roasted chicken, but I don't want to hurt other animals, so I use these instead. Just plant them in the ground, and by morning, you'll have fresh raw meat ready to cook."

The lady hugged the bear.

"Thank you so much, Mister Bear!" she said.
"I'm sorry I tried to eat you and all your friends."

So the lady went home, planted the meat seeds in her garden, and waited until morning. The next morning, she couldn't believe her eyes! Sitting in her garden were raw steaks, chickens ready to be roasted, slippery bacon strips, and many more types of meat.

"Hooray!" said the lady. "I love meat seeds!"

That day, the lady had a big feast of meat and
vegetables and invited all of the animals in the woods.

"This is a wonderful feast!" said the bear.
"Thanks for making it for us."

"I'll never try to eat any of you again," the lady
replied. "I'll be using meat seeds from now on."

Now, the lady uses meat seeds for everything, from hamburger patties to shrimp for gumbo. She even found sweet dessert seeds! She still eats vegetables too, but as side dishes.

And she is thankful to the big, brown bear that helped her find a cruelty-free source of food.

THE END

ABOUT THE AUTHOR: RHYS GRIFFIN

Rhys Griffin is not just an author, but also a voice actor, filmmaker, and videographer for Spectrum Fusion. In other words, he is a storyteller. Since childhood, Rhys has always wanted to share his stories with the world. In 2017, Rhys graduated from the University of Houston–Clear Lake with a Bachelor of Arts in Communications.

Since then, Rhys has been working with Spectrum Fusion to tell stories, be it his own or others. He has gone on to provide voiceovers for clients such as Johnson & Johnson and auditioned for an Acura commercial, receiving positive feedback. He has been fascinated with trains and sees them as comforting in his adult life. Most recently, he published his first book, Tucker and the Christmas Train, that was released in December 2020. The book received positive reviews, and the release was featured across various media outlets, including the Houston Chronicle.

ABOUT THE ILLUSTRATOR: RACHEL JOANNA

Rachel Joanna is a freelance illustrator from Louisville, Kentucky. She has been passionate about art since she was very young. Rachel graduated from the Savannah College of Art and Design with a BFA in Sequential Art, a major that focuses heavily on comics, storyboarding, concept art, and, most importantly, children's books! She hopes to have her own series of comics published in the near future. Aside from art, Rachel loves to read and listen to music. She's always working on commissioned artwork and posting her latest creations on Instagram and Twitter at RJayStreet.

Dr. Heidi Stieglitz Ham is the Chief Empowerment Officer and Founder of Spectrum Fusion (https://spectrumfusion.org/), a 501(c)(3) nonprofit organization that does just that—empowers individuals on the autism spectrum to overcome barriers and reach their full potential. She launched the Reactor Room Program, designed to create new and innovative opportunities for individuals, providing them access to important connections. Dr. Ham has a M.S. in Speech Pathology, a Ph.D. in Psychology from the University of Edinburgh, and is an adjunct professor at Rice University.

CPSIA information can be obtained
at www.ICGtesting.com
Printed in the USA
BVHW021208250122
627119BV00008B/790

9 781645 382447